HAZEL HUTCHINS and GAIL HERBERT
THE TRUTH ABOUT
WIND

Illustrated by DUŠAN PETRIČIĆ

annick press

toronto • berkeley

© 2020 Hazel Hutchins and Gail Herbert (text)
© 2020 Dušan Petričić (illustrations)
Designed by Paul Covello

Second printing, October 2020

Annick Press Ltd.
All rights reserved. No part of this work covered by the copyrights hereon may be reproduced or used in any form
or by any means—graphic, electronic, or mechanical—without the prior written permission of the publisher.

We acknowledge the support of the Canada Council for the Arts and the Ontario Arts Council, and the participation
of the Government of Canada/la participation du gouvernement du Canada for our publishing activities.

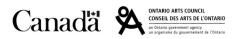

Library and Archives Canada Cataloguing in Publication

Title: The truth about wind / Hazel Hutchins and Gail Herbert ; illustrated by Dušan Petričić.
Names: Hutchins, Hazel, author. | Herbert, Gail, author. | Petričić, Dušan, illustrator.
Identifiers: Canadiana (print) 20190166088 | Canadiana (ebook) 20190166207 | ISBN 9781773213880
   (hardcover) | ISBN 9781773213910 (PDF) | ISBN 9781773213903 (Kindle) | ISBN 9781773213897 (HTML)
Classification: LCC PS8565.U826 T78 2020 | DDC jC813/.54—dc23

Published in the U.S.A. by Annick Press (U.S.) Ltd.
Distributed in Canada by University of Toronto Press.
Distributed in the U.S.A. by Publishers Group West.

Printed in China

annickpress.com
hazelhutchins.net

Also available as an e-book.
Please visit annickpress.com/ebooks for more details.

For Isaac, Theo, and Logan. Much love.
—H.H.

For Jessica, Arden, and Ben.
—G.H.

For Majda, the most joyful
baby girl in the world.
—D.P.

Jesse heard the creaking sound first.

A wagon was moving along the path behind his yard.

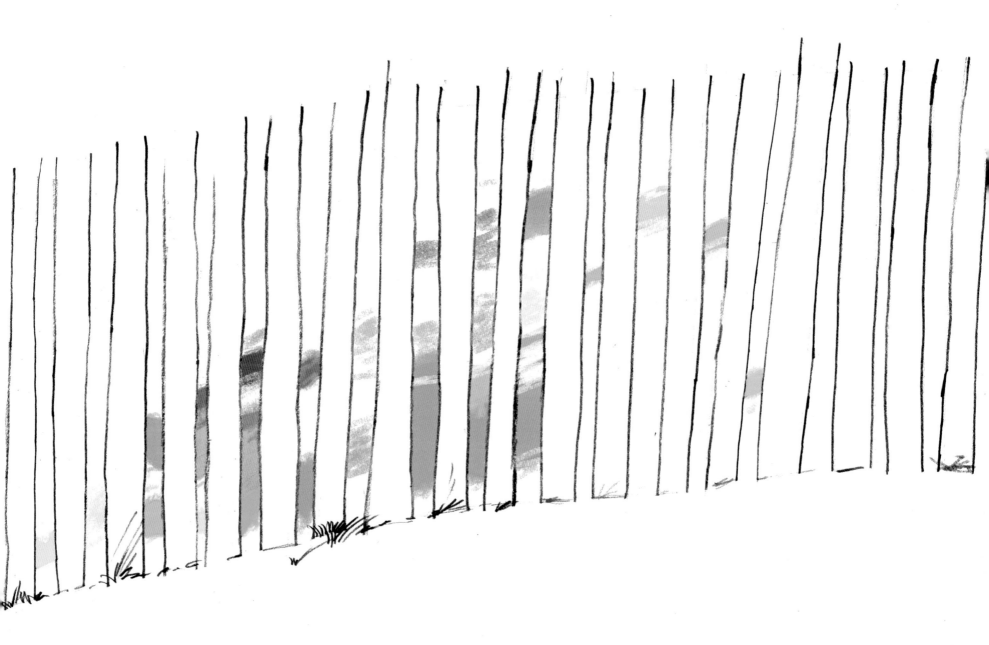

Shapes flickered beyond the fence—
a man, a girl, someone little in the wagon.

And one smaller shape that remained after the wagon had gone.

Jesse peered between the boards.

Looking brightly back at him from the tall, wild grasses was a horse—
a horse the color of a crow's wing, so shiny and black.

No one was in sight.

Jesse coaxed the horse with clover and dandelions to the safety of his yard. He built it a perfect stable beside the shed.

Jesse's mother smiled when she came
to put her gardening tools away.

"Where did you get this fine fellow?"
she asked.

"Grandma," Jesse answered quickly.

"He runs faster than any horse in the world so I have named him Wind."

Wind raced across the tabletop prairie and up and over the rolling cauliflower hills while Jesse ate supper.

He leaped deep canyons and sailed above tall waterfalls while Jesse had his bath.

"Jesse is having a wonderful time
with the horse you gave him,"
Mother told Grandmother
during their evening phone call.

"Other Grandma!"
called Jesse as Wind slid
down a soapy slope.
"From an old box!"

For there had been a box, once,
although it had never held a
shiny black horse.

Only when lying in bed, with Wind asleep
on the pillow beside him, did Jesse begin to
have an uneasy feeling in his stomach.

He pushed it away by telling the moon
the true story of an entire kingdom of wild
horses running as fast and as free as the wind.

All that week, Wind lived up to his name—galloping up the slide at the park, racing along the river path, and splashing through puddles at glorious speed.

Jesse grew to love Wind more and more.

But the uneasy feeling grew stronger.

"Snack time," Jesse suddenly told
Wind at the grocery store. He carefully
tucked the horse and a lettuce leaf into
the bottom of his backpack.

And at the library, where Wind galloped down the hall to send the posters on the message board fluttering, Jesse quickly turned him back to the safety of the shelves.

"It's better here," explained Jesse. "We can play hide-and-seek."

Each day now, Jesse became more watchful.

"Jesse has decided there's a troll living
under the bridge," Mother said with a sigh
on her evening phone call to Grandmother.
"We had to walk home the long way around."

Then other Grandmother called.
Mother handed Jesse the phone and whispered, "Say thank you."

Jesse had to think quickly.

"The box, Grandma. From a long time ago. I found a horse in it! Thank you."

He handed the phone back to Mother and added, "I had to remind her. You know how Grandma forgets things."

But Wind's head had lowered as Jesse spoke and they could no longer meet each other's eyes.

At supper, Jesse found it hard to swallow the spaghetti he loved.

All evening, his stomach was sore.

"You're happy here with me, aren't you, Wind?"
asked Jesse at bedtime.

Wind did not answer.

"Do you want to hear more about the true
kingdom of horses, Moon?" asked Jesse.

The moon stayed silent in the sky.

When Jesse finally fell asleep his dreams broke into shifting pieces like shapes flickering beyond a wooden fence.

And in the quietest, darkest time of night Jesse found himself awake and thinking about where Wind had really come from.

The next morning, even when Jesse offered
berries from his cereal bowl and built the most
tempting racecourse around the milk carton,
Wind stood unmoving beside Jesse's cup.

"Your horse is very quiet today.
What's wrong, Jesse?"
His mother's voice was gentle.

But how could he ever explain?

"Not hungry," said Jesse. And he slipped away to the backyard.

He sat. And sat.

And then—far down the path—came the creaking sound of the wagon.

It had been there most mornings but Jesse had pretended not to hear.
This time, however, he turned to Wind saying, "You hear it too, don't you?"

He already knew the answer.

Jesse gave Wind one enormous last hug.

He hurried to the fence.

He forced himself to hold the horse as far as he could toward the people on the path.

A single word rang into the air.

"Midnight!"

It was a name so perfect, and said with such joy, that Jesse's sadness and confusion suddenly fell away. The girl ran forward.

"You found my horse! You found Midnight!"

And the shiny black horse—dark as midnight, fast as wind—raced home.